The Giant Sunflower

Diane Marwood

A fantasy story

First published in 2011 by
Franklin Watts
338 Euston Road
London NW1 3BH

Franklin Watts Australia
Level 17/207 Kent Street
Sydney NSW 2000

A CIP catalogue record for this book is
available from the British Library.

ISBN: 978 1 4451 0410 2 (hbk)
ISBN: 978 1 4451 0419 5 (pbk)

Illustrations by Artful Doodlers Ltd.
Art Director: Jonathan Hair
Series Editor: Jackie Hamley
Series Designer: Matthew Lilly

Printed in China

Franklin Watts is a division of
Hachette Children's Books,
an Hachette UK company.
www.hachette.co.uk

There was a competition at school to grow the tallest sunflower.
Everyone planted a seed.

"I'll win!" said Kim.
"No, I will!" said Ash.
Polly laughed.

Every day, Kim and Ash ran to see if their sunflowers had grown. There were two tiny shoots.

But Polly's sunflower had grown so tall that she could not see the top!

"I'll climb it first!" said Kim. "No, I will!" cried Ash.

Kim and
Ash started
to climb...

higher and
higher...

... until they found
a land above
the clouds.

Kim and Ash saw
two giant feet!
"Argh!" they
screamed.

Then they heard a deep,
loud rumble.

Kim and Ash ran
and hid under
a huge daisy.
"How do we get
down?" asked Ash.

"We need to find Polly's sunflower without the giant finding us!" Kim replied.

Suddenly, there was a loud buzz. An enormous bee hovered above them. "Jump!" shouted Ash.

Ash and Kim grabbed
hold of the bee.

They held on tight as the bee swooped through different flowers.

At last, it landed on Polly's sunflower.

Ash and Kim let go and
quickly climbed down.

"Who won?"
asked Polly.

Polly

"You won!" laughed Kim and Ash. "Your sunflower is a giant!"

Puzzles

Which speech bubbles belong to Ash?

Which words describe Kim
and which describe the giant?

excited

cross

happy

grumpy

hungry

thrilled

Answers

Ash's speech bubbles are: 1, 3, 4

Kim is: excited, happy, thrilled.
The giant is: cross, grumpy, hungry.

Espresso Connections

This book may be used in conjunction with the Science area on Espresso to start a discussion on plant growth.

It may also be used to inspire a creative writing activity. Here are some suggestions.

Growth

Talk about what plants need to grow well – light and water. In the pictures of this story, can they see any reasons why Polly's sunflower has grown more than Ash's or Kim's sunflower?

Visit the Growing Plants section in Science 1. Open the Things to do and choose the plant growth activity sheet. Ask children to complete the sheet drawing the growth of the plant.

You could also use the activity sheets on Plants and water and Plants and sunlight in conjunction with experiments on growth.

Write your own adventure story

Visit the Story starts section in English 1, and open "Scary story: The Enormous Flower".

Watch the video together, and ask the children what they think it would be like to have a plant this big and smelly in their garden.

Open the book activity and read the beginning of the book together.

Ask the children to think about what will happen next. Discuss the possible options – Where will the flower grow to?

Visit the "Writing resource box" in English 1, and go to the Activity arcade. Choose the "Writing frame" activity and select "Story – adventure" on the left. Tab through the information that is given about this genre.

Decide together on the opening of your adventure story, then on the problem(s), the events and the ending. Then perfect your class story in the writing frame, using the word bank on the left to edit and improve it.